# West by Steamboat

## Tim McNeese

**Crestwood House**
New York

Maxwell Macmillan Canada
Toronto

Maxwell Macmillan International
New York   Oxford   Singapore   Sydney

Design and production: Deborah Fillion
Illustrations: © Chris Duke

Crestwood House
Macmillan Publishing Company
866 Third Avenue
New York, NY 10022

Maxwell Macmillan Canada, Inc.
1200 Eglinton Avenue East
Suite 200
Don Mills, Ontario M3C 3N1

Macmillan Publishing Company is part of the
Maxwell Communication Group of Companies.

First edition

Printed in the United States of America

10 9 8 7 6 5 4 3 2 1

**Library of Congress Cataloging-in-Publication Data**

McNeese, Tim.
    West by steamboat / by Tim McNeese.— 1st ed.
       p.   cm. — (Americans on the move)
    Summary: Discusses westward expansion prior to the Civil War and the role of the steamboats on the inland rivers in the settlement of the West.
    ISBN 0-89686-728-5
    1. West (U. S.)—Description and travel—to 1848—Juvenile literature.
2. West (U. S.)—Description and travel—1848-1860—Juvenile literature.
3. River steamers—West (U. S.)—History—19th century—Juvenile literature.
[1. West (U. S.)—History. 2. River steamers—West (U. S.)—History. I. Title.
II. Series: McNeese, Tim. Americans on the move.
F592.M35 1993
978'.02—dc20                                 91-22822

★

# Contents

★

# Introduction

In the early 1800s Americans began to move west by the thousands. These early pioneers had only a few travel choices. Most of them traveled by wagon or on foot. Many, however, traveled west on the water. They floated down the many rivers that **crisscross** the lands west of the Appalachian Mountains.

The Ohio River was an important water route for early pioneers. In time the great Mississippi River would become a major "trail" for westerners. This river would connect the interior of the new nation with the port of New Orleans. Other rivers, from the Tennessee to the Missouri, the Arkansas to the Wabash, would become part of the huge western river system used by Americans on the move.

At first western settlers, traders, trappers and farmers used a variety of oar- and current-propelled boats to get from one place to another. Canoes, flat-boats and keelboats were common on the western rivers long before the invention of the first steamboat. But once steam was harnessed to produce power, the rivers became two-way streets. With this new invention, men and women could go upstream against the river currents just as fast as they could travel downstream.

*With the invention of the steamboat, American pioneers were
able to journey to new and exciting parts of the country.*

Although the first steamboats built in the United
States were used on eastern rivers like the Hudson in
New York State, it did not take long before someone built
a steamboat on a western river. Beginning with that first
western steamboat and for the next half century, the
western rivers became filled with steam-powered craft.
This new age, the age of the western river steamboat,
helped bring people and prosperity to the West.

★

*Early American steamboats like Roosevelt's*
*New Orleans opened up a whole new world*
*of travel and adventure to western settlers.*

# Nicholas Roosevelt and the First Western Steamer

onstruction of the first western river steamboat began in 1810. The boat was launched a year later in March 1811. This steamboat was 138 feet long and cost about $40,000. It could carry 371 tons of cargo. No one knows whether its paddle wheel, which propelled it through the water, was on the side or along the back, also called the stern.

Nicholas J. Roosevelt laid the keel for his boat in the spring near the then western city of Pittsburgh. He did this because in Pittsburgh the Monongahela and the Allegheny Rivers join together to form the Ohio River. The Ohio River flows to the southwest and empties into the mighty Mississippi River.

When he finished building the boat, Roosevelt steamed it up the Monongahela to show that his steamboat could do what steamboats had to do: Travel against a river's current. Because the waters of the Ohio were too shallow at the time, Roosevelt could not head down this river until October. By then he was ready to steam down-river to the great western territories.

In these early years of travel west of the Appalachian Mountains, the Ohio River valley was not well populated. From Pittsburgh to Louisville, Kentucky, there were people scattered all along the Ohio. The same was true of the Mississippi from the port of New Orleans to the town of Natchez, in Mississippi. The riverbank from Louisville to Natchez—over 1,100 miles—was mostly uninhabited. Louisville itself had only 1,500 people. Only small settlements that clung to the river could be found between the two cities.

Roosevelt arrived in Louisville, Kentucky, late one night and awakened the townspeople with the boat's whis-tle. Few of these people had ever seen a steamboat. For several days Roosevelt gave the settlers rides on his steamboat, which he had named the *New Orleans*. His wife accompanied him on this exciting journey, as well as the family dog, a Newfoundland named Tiger.

At that time the river narrowed at Louisville at what was known as the Falls or Chutes of the Ohio. Actually more rapids than waterfalls, the waters there were too low to allow the *New Orleans* to pass through safely. So Roosevelt spent his time traveling from Louisville back to Cincinnati, which lay upriver.

The river finally rose high enough to allow the *New Orleans* to squeeze through the Chutes. This part of the trip was dangerous. There are stories of how even Tiger became frightened and quietly sat through the whole scene at Mrs. Roosevelt's feet. But the *New Orleans* was able to get through safely and Roosevelt continued his trip down to the Mississippi. He and his wife hoped for a quiet trip down to the mouth of the great river and a heralded arrival in the port of New Orleans.

★

Under normal conditions, perhaps the trip might have been a peaceful one. But the year 1811 in the Ohio valley was anything but peaceful. The spring floods changed the flow of the western rivers. A great comet was appearing in the night sky, arousing western settlers' superstitions. It was also the year of the strange Great Squirrel Migration, when, for no known reason, thousands of gray squirrels began swimming across the Ohio to the southern shore. Most of them did not make it.

## The New Madrid Earthquake

The years 1811 and 1812 were also notable for the New Madrid Earthquake. The center of this immense earthquake was New Madrid, Missouri, a tiny settlement in the southern corner of the territory along the banks of the Mississippi. This set off a series of violent earthquakes which were the strongest on record in North America. Although the earthquake was centered in the southern Missouri and Memphis, Tennessee, area, its effects could be felt hundreds of miles away in eastern cities. Stories are told of how the quake caused church bells to ring in Boston and plaster walls to crack in Baltimore. And the unfortunate Nicholas Roosevelt, his wife, their new baby and Tiger found themselves in the middle of it.

For two weeks as the *New Orleans* steamed its way south, the great river began to churn, the water leaping into heavy waves. Riverbanks slid into the choppy waters and rock bluffs toppled down. In some places the Mississippi lost its channel and, for a time, actually rolled backward. Reelfoot Lake, near Memphis, was formed during the earthquake. On land the earth itself moved in waves and ripples. Trees snapped apart.

One night the *New Orleans* was tied to a tree on a river island. The next morning Roosevelt found the rope still tied to the tree. But the island had disappeared down into the river, taking the tree with it. The rope led into the mysterious depths of the quickly-changing river.

# A Successful Voyage

Despite all the first shocks and many aftershocks of the giant earthquake, the Roosevelts kept going. Down the river went the *New Orleans*, steaming past destroyed villages and settlements, dodging floating trees and stumps. In mid-January the *New Orleans* reached the city of New Orleans. For the first time in history a steamboat had traveled from Pittsburgh down the Ohio to the Mississippi River and then to the great Louisiana port.

But the story of the *New Orleans* does not end there. For the next two years the steamboat was used in the river trade between New Orleans and Natchez, Mississippi. In fact this is the trade area for which the *New Orleans* had been built, working the broad lower river. During these years the boat earned enough to pay for its construction and operating costs, plus a tidy profit.

One July night in 1814, the *New Orleans* was working in the area of Baton Rouge where it was tied up to take on wood. The next morning, when steam was raised to move the paddle wheels, the boat would not budge. During the night the river's water level had dropped, and the hull of the *New Orleans* was sitting on an underwater stump.

As the boat's engineer tried to work the boat free, the stump pushed a hole through the hull, flooding the boiler room. The passengers barely had time to escape from the sinking steamboat. There the story of the first of the Mississippi steamers reaches its sad ending.

# Others Follow the *New Orleans*

The success of Nicholas Roosevelt and the *New Orleans* ushered in a new era of many river steamboats allowing trade and travel to the western settlers and pioneers.

The second western river steamer was the *Comet*. This boat was built near Brownsville, Pennsylvania, on the Ohio River in 1813. In 1814 the *Comet* came downriver to New Orleans. It would make two trips upriver to Natchez before the boat was dismantled and her engine used in a southern cotton factory.

Many other boats were built in Pittsburgh. Some of the early ones were the *Vesuvius* (which would be the third steamboat on the Mississippi), the *Aetna*, the *Buffalo* and even a second *New Orleans*. These boats were paid for by the same men who had provided money to Nicholas Roosevelt to build the first ship.

These early followers of the first *New Orleans* enjoyed some similar successes, but soon met with disaster. The *Vesuvius* reached New Orleans in the spring of 1814. But on the trip back upriver the ship grounded on a

Memphis sandbar. There it stayed for six months until the high waters of December eased it free. On the return trip to New Orleans the *Vesuvius* grounded again, this time for ten more weeks. Its days were ended in 1815, when it was destroyed in a fire.

The *Aetna* performed well through 1815 and 1816, steaming between Louisville and the lower Mississippi. But by the end of 1816, the *Aetna* had broken both paddle-wheel shafts, putting the boat out of service.

The *Buffalo* was designed to be an Ohio boat, built to run even during the low-water months of summer. But this boat's problems would be financial, not physical. Unpaid debts on the *Buffalo* caused it to be sold at a sheriff's sale in Louisville. Despite its size and the quality of its **staterooms** and cabins (it had comfortable rooms for over 100 passengers), the *Buffalo* was sold for only $800.

Many other boats would follow in the years to come. By 1817, 14 steamers had found their way to the Ohio and Mississippi.

★

*The great Louisiana port of New Orleans was a major stop for steamboats that traveled on the Mississippi.*

## St. Louis Sees Its First Steamer

In 1817 the first steamer chugged up the Mississippi to St. Louis. The *Zebulon M. Pike* had been built in Henderson, Kentucky. It was a small boat with a low-pressure engine. The crew had to help the boat get upriver by pushing poles against the current, as was the practice on keelboats. The *Pike* reached St. Louis on a hot August day, and everyone in town came out to see the new river machine. Its life was a short one, however. The next year the *Pike* hit a snag on the Red River and promptly sank.

By 1819, 31 steamboats were in operation between Louisville and New Orleans. All told, over 60 steamboats were in use on western rivers by 1819. Before the end of the 19th century, over 4,000 steamboats would work the western rivers, most of them passing through the port at New Orleans.

# From the Cumberland to the Arkansas

After 1811 and the successful first voyage of the *New Orleans*, many steamers took their turns on other western rivers. These first boats were small boats with only one deck. And their early trips found them not only on the broad reaches of the Mississippi, but on many other rivers of the Ohio-Mississippi River valley.

In 1818 a boat called the *General Jackson* paddled up the Cumberland River from New Orleans and landed in Nashville. In 1821 a small steamer, the *Osage*, struggled up the Tennessee River. Within six years a dozen boats were running regularly out of the Tennessee capital.

North of the Ohio River is the Wabash River, where steamboats could be found by the late 1820s. The first steamers on the Arkansas River were military transports taking supplies to Arkansas posts. Two years later a steamboat docked at Little Rock.

Within a few years of the first Mississippi trip of the steamboat *New Orleans*, steamboats were beginning to make their way up the Missouri River. The first was in 1819 when the *Independence* ran up the Missouri to the frontier settlement of Franklin, at the beginning of the Santa Fe Trail. It had taken the *Independence* 13 days to make the trip; seven of those days were spent aground. One of the witnesses to the arrival of the *Independence* in Franklin was a ten-year-old boy named Kit Carson, who grew up to be a famous western guide, explorer and scout. Days later the little steamer paddled up to the Chariton River, about 250 miles across the territory of Missouri.

Steamboats quickly became fairly common on the lower Missouri. But for several decades the upper river was the far western highway for trappers, hunters and U.S. Army units. The hostility of Indians like the Crow and Sioux kept settlers out of the upper Missouri River country.

★

Many upper Missouri boats faced Indian attacks. Most pilothouses were protected by iron plating. Sometimes Indians would attack the boats, then take to their ponies and ride upstream. There they would lie in wait for the next river passengers.

Boats that followed the *Independence* went a little farther up the river each year until, in 1860, a steamboat made the trip to Fort Benton, Montana. This was as far as steamboats could travel: 2,200 miles up the Missouri River.

The best years for steamboat trade on the Missouri River were between 1855 and 1860. Fifty-nine steamboats were steaming up and down the lower Missouri by 1858. The next year the records show more steamboats leaving St. Louis and heading up the Missouri than leaving the city for a Mississippi voyage.

Taking a steamboat up the Missouri was never easy. The Missouri was a thick, muddy river that was always changing course. There were many sandbars and the river was very wild when the spring floods came. During the dry season the river was often too low for safe navigation with a steamboat. Those boats that did travel the Missouri were mostly stern-wheelers, because the river was sometimes not wide enough during low water for side-wheelers.

## Cotton Is King on the Mississippi

Despite the valuable trade in the 1850s on the Missouri River, the lower Mississippi was still the busiest river in the nation. Cotton was the chief reason. So much cotton was grown in the southern states by that time that the boats stacked it up on all available deck space during the picking season. These lower Mississippi steamboats were the stuff of steaming legend. These boats, especially the passenger packets, with their fancy rooms and expensive

*Because most of America's cotton was grown in the South, the lower Mississippi was the river most often used for trade.*

furnishings, helped create the romance of river travel during the ten years before the Civil War.

These were the days of little shipping competition along the rivers, except among boats. The railroads were just beginning to snake their way to the Mississippi. Freight wagons were expensive. Most boats turned handsome profits before they exploded, sank or were retired from the river trade.

By the 1850s and even earlier, many of the river hazards were gone. Specially designed boats called **snag boats** had been built to clear the rivers of stumps, half-submerged trees and other obstacles. Many places along the rivers, from the Tennessee to the Arkansas, were made safer with the removal of these river problems.

★

# Steamers Change and Grow

O ver the first 40 years of steamboat travel on the western rivers, steamers in America changed in size, power, design and construction. But it took only about 20 years of western river steaming before the boats began to look pretty much like the boats of the golden era of steamboating, from the late 1840s until the beginning of the Civil War in 1861.

## Floating Palaces

Riverboats were made, at least on the outside, of wood. The hull was usually made of oak or some other hard-wood. But most of the boat above the waterline was made of softwood, like pine.

With each passing year new boats were built and improved. They became bigger, they could carry more cargo and passengers and they could travel faster. The early steamers were plain boats, usually flat with a paddle wheel on one side. Passenger cabins were small and

★

cramped. People took their meals in small eating rooms at both ends of the boat, one for men, one for women.

Between 1830 and 1840 steamboats became big and gaudy. They had several decks, each of which was decorated with lots of fancy woodwork and gingerbread designs.

Nearly all Mississippi steamboats were painted

*The highly decorated boats built between 1830 and 1840 looked like elaborate works of art.*

white. On some boats the wooden trim was painted red or blue. On side-wheelers, the paddle boxes covering the wheels were painted many different ways. A painter would often create a sunburst, because it easily fit the half-circle space. But other subjects were painted. On a boat called the *Ben Franklin*, the paddle box sported Franklin flying his famous kite.

Between 1830 and 1840 boats began to boast elaborate ornaments and gingerbread woodwork. Natchez boats usually had a bale of cotton painted on the paddle box. Still others had patterns of stars, anchors, globes and other designs.

## The Steamers Down Below

Most steamboats had their machinery on the main deck. The boilers were placed in front of the boat's engines. Many of the western steamboats had passenger space on the main deck and toward the front of the boat or above the boilers. Other cabins lined the boiler deck.

Inside the boat's hold was the freight and cargo. The main deck held the engines, boilers, kitchen and passengers' cabins. All other available room was given to additional freight. On the boiler deck was the boat's office, where the captain usually took care of his steamer's business. The barroom, staterooms and the women's cabins were also on the boiler deck. Staterooms were expensive passenger cabins, and often these cabins were named for a state in the Union. Staircases led up from the forward part of the main deck. This part of the boat was called the **forecastle**. Around the outline of the steamer was a walkway called the **promenade**.

Above all this was the hurricane deck, where the pilothouse and the officers' cabin were located. This cabin was called the Texas because, just as the state of Texas was a later addition to the nation, it was added to later steamboat designs.

The Texas was a boxy extension behind the pilot-house. At first this addition served as living quarters for the boat's officers. Later passengers were sometimes housed there. Two huge smokestacks generally capped off the boat's design, perhaps making the boat appear larger.

In comparison to the early steamboats, western steamers soon became elaborate floating palaces. On many of the later boats the saloon was a fancy place indeed. There the furniture was expensive and often imported from Europe. The carpets were the best of the textile mills of Brussels. Ceilings shone with gilded tiles and stained-glass windows added light and color. Elaborate chandeliers of shiny cut glass lit up the saloons. Silver **spittoons** lined the saloon floor.

## Carrying People and Prosperity

In the early decades of steamboating on the western rivers, the boats carried lots of different kinds of cargo. Between 1810 and 1840 they carried many emigrants into the western lands to settle and start farms and shops. Farm produce was soon making its way to market by steamboat. Much of the western produce went down to New Orleans, where it was sold. The fur trade in the upper Louisiana Territory lured steamboats up the Missouri and Yellowstone rivers. This made the town of St. Louis a very important river community.

When the settlers headed west in the 1830s and 1840s, St. Louis grew rapidly. In 1819 the population of St. Louis stood at 4,000. After Missouri became a state in 1821 and the wagon trade along the Santa Fe Trail opened up, business in St. Louis mushroomed. A major part of that trade was due to the steamboat. In 1822 the amount

★

*The saloon was usually the fanciest part of the steamboat.*

★

of freight passing through St. Louis weighed in at 15,000 pounds. Within 20 years the total of St. Louis cargo reached half a million pounds.

## Sudden Death Aboard a Steamer

Steamboating was always a dangerous business. There were many ways to bring "sudden death to a steamboat." The average river life of a steamboat on the Mississippi was about five years. Speed was always a problem. Pilots and captains alike would order their boat's fireboxes stuffed with fuel. Often they would throw in oil or turpentine to fan the flames. Steam-pressure safety valves were sometimes tied down, allowing the boilers to reach dangerously high pressures. Higher pressure caused the machinery to work faster, speeding the boat along.

Fire itself was always a danger. All riverboats were made of wood—lots of it, from hull to pilothouse—and a careless little fire could set the whole boat aflame. Sparks were always flying from a boat's tall smokestacks, threatening to turn the boat to tinder. Sometimes cargo was loaded in such a way as to cause a fire hazard. Cotton bales could catch on fire from showers of sparks. Dangerous cargo such as gunpowder was sometimes packed on a boat as if it were kegs of nails or salt pork, with no special precautions. Cargo was often packed in straw, which could be set ablaze by a careless passenger's cigar.

## The Golden Age of Steamboating

By the 1840s the steamboat river trade was reaching its golden age. From that time until the beginning of the Civil War in 1861, steamboats caused the western territories and states to grow rapidly. The cotton trade boomed. In 1811 Tennessee, Mississippi and Louisiana had exported

★

five million pounds of cotton. Thirty years later these states exported 200 million pounds of the white fiber. By 1843 the port of New Orleans was the busiest in the country, handling twice the tonnage of New York's harbor. In the 1850s the steamboat trade had become a booming business. And legends and stories were already being told about the great Mississippi steamers and packets that carried people up and down the great river.

# The *Eclipse:*
# One of the Mississippi's Best

There were many great steamboats on the Mississippi in the 1850s. One example of what steamboats had become by that time was an outstanding boat called the *Eclipse*. The *Eclipse* was a very fast boat. In 1853 it made a run from New Orleans to Louisville in four days, nine hours and 31 minutes.

The *Eclipse* was a giant steamer, measuring 363 feet long and 36 feet wide with a hold nine feet deep. It boasted two engines with 36-inch cylinders. These were fueled by eight boilers, each measuring over 32 feet in length. Its paddle wheel measured 41 feet in diameter. Its paddle buckets were 14 feet long and over two feet wide.

Inside, the *Eclipse* was a dream boat. The cabins were decorated with gilt furnishings. Oil paintings lined the long hall. Two great statues stood at either end of the hall, one of Andrew Jackson and one of Henry Clay. A piano provided the passengers with music. The boat carried a crew of 121 and there were cabins for 180 passengers. Those couples recently married had their choice of 48 different bridal rooms!

And the amazing thing is that the *Eclipse* was, during the 1850s, only one of many New Orleans packets like it!

★

# Men of the River

In the days of the Mississippi steamboats, those men who worked the boats, from the captain on down to the deckhands, or **roustabouts**, were viewed with high regard. There were several important jobs to be done on a steamboat.

Naturally, the most glorified job was that of captain. On western rivers like the Mississippi and Missouri, the

*Steamboats were often destroyed by river sandbars.*

captain usually owned his steamboat. He made it his business to keep in touch with nearly everything that kept his boat going. He regularly checked on the machinery and paid the fuel and repair bills. He ordered food for the kitchen. He made business deals that provided goods and freight for his boat to carry. And he had to be friendly with the passengers in order to keep them happy.

But for all the captain had to do on a steamboat, it was the pilot who steered the craft. While the captain had to know everything there was to know about his steamboat, the pilot had to know everything there was to know about the river. He had to memorize the many **channels**, the depth of water at innumerable crossings and when to make those crossings. He had constant worries with such unseen river threats as snags, sandbars and **sawyers**. Sawyers are logs or trees stuck in the river, so called because the branches would saw back and forth with the current. The pilot also had to keep in touch with the engi-

★

neer in the engine room at all times. It was his duty to keep on schedule as much as was humanly possible. He also had the responsibility for the lives of all the passengers and crew onboard.

In the early days of riverboating, pilots had to know how to stay in the deepest and safest water. To determine

*The riverboat pilot was required to know every detail about the river in order to get his passengers to their destinations in a safe and timely manner.*

the water's depth, pilots relied on a roustabout called a **leadsman**. When the pilot wanted a water sounding, he would tap a big bell. The leadsman would immediately come on deck carrying a long rope with a lead weight tied to the end. The rope would have knots the same length apart. The leadsman would heave the rope into the water. From this he could measure the depth of the water, telling the pilot whether the channel was deep enough for passage or whether the water was getting shallow.

The leadsman would holler out the water's depth: "mark one" (six feet), "quarter less one" ($4\frac{1}{2}$ feet), "quarter twain" ($13\frac{1}{2}$ feet), "quarter one" ($7\frac{1}{2}$ feet). Of course, the most famous cry of the leadsman was "mark twain," meaning two **fathoms** of water (12 feet), which was considered very safe water for steamboats. The famous writer Samuel Clemens used "Mark Twain" as his pen name. He wrote such works as *Tom Sawyer, Huckleberry Finn* and a book about his own experiences on the big river as a pilot in training, *Life on the Mississippi.*

Then there was the engine-room crew. These men lived with the heavy machinery amid the great furnaces and the hissing boilers that gave the great steamboats their power. The engineer would watch the pressure gauges to insure that the boat was traveling safely—without the threat of explosion.

The engineer would adjust the speed and direction of the vessel as the pilot gave him orders. Often these instructions came through a speaking tube that ran from the pilothouse down to the noisy engine room. **Stokers**, often free blacks, had to feed the furnace fires by shoveling in wood or coal. Their job was a backbreaking one. In addition the heat of the furnace room kept these furnace "firemen" sweating through their shifts. Many steamboats had as many as ten boilers, providing high-pressure steam to the boat's engines.

On deck steamboats relied on the roustabouts. Their job was the loading and unloading of hundreds of crates, barrels and bales of freight each day. Often they would rest between stops, but as soon as a steamboat tied up during a run, the roustabouts would jump to their work. They carried cargo on and off—everything from bales of cotton to barrels of gunpowder to kegs of whiskey. The roustabouts had to work fast and hard to help keep the steamboat on schedule.

And to keep them on their toes, all steamboats had a worker called a mate. The mate was generally a hard-driving man who hollered at the roustabouts to pick up their loads and step lively. Mates often had booming voices, and threatened the roustabouts if they thought they were not carrying their weight.

## River Stories and Superstitions

The men who worked the western rivers had their own stories, legends and superstitions about river life and steamboat travel. Black roustabouts held many strange beliefs about what would bring good and bad luck to a riverman. It was believed, for example, that washing one's face in the river would bring good luck. Throwing any animal or bird into the river was bad luck. Having a gray mare and a preacher onboard a steamboat at the same time was definitely bad luck. The famous writer Mark Twain even included that superstition in his book about steamboating on the "Big Muddy," *Life on the Mississippi*.

Perhaps the most well-known river legend centered on a mythical creature named Old Al. Black roustabouts talked with great respect and fear about Old Al, a gigantic alligator along the lower reaches of the Mississippi. Old Al smoked a pipe and changed the course of the river by dragging his tail to make new channels. He was the king of

*Old Al, king of the alligators, was one of many legends among the men of the river.*

the alligators. When he puffed heavily on his pipe, he created thick fog that hung on the river, forcing steamboats to tie up. He was even rumored occasionally to snatch a roustabout off a steamboat deck and down him for lunch.

★

# Wood Fuels the Steamboats

To keep these giants of the river going, the hundreds of boats required great amounts of fuel. Either coal or wood was used to power the ships. Such fuel for steamboats was always plentiful. The rivers were lined with trees. And the steamboats burned a great deal of wood. Even a small steamboat would burn as many as 20 to 30 **cords** a day. (A cord is a common measurement for a stack of cut wood: four-by-four-by-eight-feet.)

In the early days of steamboating, steamboat crews would go into the woods twice daily to cut such hardwoods as oak, beech, chestnut, maple and ash to burn in the boat's furnaces.

As more steamboats came to the Mississippi, men living along the river built wood lots or yards. These riverside farmers could make a regular income from selling wood to steamboats. Wood was generally stacked in ranks which measured eight feet high by four feet wide and stretched 84 feet in length. Each rank held 20 cords.

Woodcutting became a big business. Steamboat captains usually paid $2.50 for a cord of wood. A large wood yard in Mississippi once boasted 20,000 cords of cut wood. This wood was worth between $50,000 and $70,000.

Hardwoods made good fuel and were plentiful along the Ohio River and the upper Mississippi. Cottonwood, a softwood, was used on the lower Mississippi. It burned hot and very quickly. Along the lower regions of the big river, pine was burned and was for many steamboat engineers their favorite wood. Pine burned hot and was loaded with flammable resin or sap.

Sometimes boats needed to load up wood at night. To alert a nearby wood yard, a boat pilot would ring a signal bell. This would alert lot keepers of an approaching

★

*Fueling a steamboat required a great deal of wood
and many crew members to gather it.*

boat that needed wood. The keeper would light a pre-
pared bonfire to let his wood yard be seen in the dark.
"Wooding up" under cover of darkness was eerie and
thrilling, since it was done by the jumpy light of torches
and bonfires.

With the coming of the western steamboats, millions of trees were burned for fuel. As the trees were cut,
towns and farms were built in the newly-opened places.
Wood would continue to be the common fuel of steamboats until after the Civil War. By then many steamers
burned coal.

★

# Towns Grow along the Rivers

N
early all the original settlements along the Mississippi River valley were connected to an important river system. During the days of the steamboats, some of these villages and small communities became important ports. Some sleepy river towns never grew, and when the river changed course some settlements found themselves miles from the water.

The greatest river city on the Mississippi was New Orleans. Located at the mouth of the great river, New Orleans was founded by the French in 1718. The city became Spanish territory and was then returned to the French. Napoleon, the French emperor, sold the city and the large territory of Louisiana to America in 1803.

Because of its French roots, New Orleans was different from nearly all other American cities. Many people spoke French and dressed differently than most other Americans. Many of the buildings looked like those in France and French Canada. There were Catholic priests and nuns, wealthy sugar **plantation** owners and many slaves being bought and sold.

★

With the growth in the number of steamboats on the Mississippi, New Orleans grew very quickly. And so did its port. In 1801 the value of the goods passing through the port of New Orleans was about $4 million. Fifty years later the value was set at almost $100 million. During the 1840s New Orleans handled twice the goods that passed through the port of New York.

As a river city New Orleans also had its problems. Because of its open sewers and poor drainage, disease was common. One part of the city was called the swamp and many river pirates and criminals stayed there. This part of town was filled with saloons and gambling dens. For many years, nearly a murder a day was committed in the swamp.

Another important Mississippi River city was Natchez, Mississippi. The settlement began life as a French fort in 1716. It was built along river cliffs that stretched 200 feet straight up from the river. Indians had originally lived there, as well as buffalo. The site became the jumping-off place for the Natchez Trace, an old Indian trail that became the major route used by flatboatmen and travelers from Tennessee. With the Natchez Trace and the Mississippi, old Natchez could boast two important travel routes.

Many large cotton plantations sprang up around Natchez during the early 1800s, making the town wealthy. Some of the most elegant mansions in the South were built around the city. Steamboats as well as flatboats stopped at Natchez. The city developed its own seamy riverfront, called Natchez-under-the-Hill, along Silver Street. Saloons and gambling halls stayed open all night. Fights and brawls, as well as robberies and murders, were common. In 1840 a great tornado tore Natchez-under-the-Hill to pieces. In the following years the river current began to eat away at the mud shelf on which Natchez-under-the-Hill

★

was located. By the 1850s Natchez-under-the-Hill had vanished, the river taking its place.

North of Natchez, along the Tennessee shore of the Mississippi, was Memphis. Like Natchez, it was also located along high bluffs. Memphis was founded in 1819 by three men, one of whom was General Andrew Jackson. During the early 1800s the settlement became one of the largest slave markets in the central South. Slave traders brought slaves upriver from New Orleans and sold them to plantation owners. By 1860 Memphis was a city of 23,000, making it the sixth largest in the South.

While some important towns sprang up because of their location on the Mississippi, others continued to be important communities even after the river itself had changed course. Vicksburg, Mississippi, is a good example. During the Civil War the city of Vicksburg gained fame as an important Confederate fortress blocking the North's advance up the Mississippi. The city was subjected to a Union **siege** and bombardment during the summer of 1863, and it fell to the North on July 4.

In 1876 Vicksburg faced another kind of problem. The Mississippi River changed course, breaking through an oxbow curve. This change in the river left this important city three miles from the Mississippi. No longer could steamboats reach Vicksburg. But the problem was solved when U.S. Army engineers changed the course of the Yazoo River to flow by Vicksburg once more. The Yazoo drained into the Mississippi, and Vicksburg became a port city again.

*Some of the most elegant mansions in the South could be found in the city of Natchez.*

★

# Racing up the River

O ne of the great advantages of a steamboat, aside from its ability to travel against a river's current, was its speed. Steamboat companies and individual boats kept exact records about travel time between cities, such as Natchez to St. Louis or New Orleans to Vicksburg and so on.

To show which boats were the fastest on the Ohio

and Mississippi rivers, pairs of gilded deer horns were given to those boats that held speed records. The horns were often mounted near the pilothouse for all to see. As long as a boat could "hold the horns" it was prized as a fast vessel. But as soon as another steamboat beat the existing record, that boat was given the deer horns. Holding the horns was not just a matter of pride on any steamboat. It also meant more business. Generally those boats known for their speed would attract the most freight and passengers.

With speed always on their minds, many steamboat pilots were often tempted to race other boats. All that was needed for such a race was that two evenly-matched steamers occupy the same stretch of river. Pilots would order up more steam, smoke would cloud the river and passengers would take to the deck railings. There they would cheer encouragement to the pilot and crew.

These unplanned races were very dangerous. Racing required more steam. More steam meant hotter furnaces. And hotter furnaces meant dangerous levels of

*Steamboat races were exciting events that attracted attention from the passengers as well as the crew.*                    ★

pressure on engine boilers. Thousands of people would lose their lives from boiler explosions, but the temptation was always there for proud pilots to show they could not be outdone by another steamer.

Some steamboat races were planned. On occasion well-known boats would give advance notice that they would be racing. Such planned races allowed each boat to prepare for the exciting event. Crews would remove all unnecessary weight from their boats. The boats would plan on stopping only at the bigger river towns, and then only if the race didn't seem close. Passengers were discouraged because they slowed the boats down.

Very special and tricky arrangements had to be made for refueling. Often wood barges would be waiting ahead, and when the racing boat came along, the barge would be tied to the boat. This cut down on idle time, for the wood was unloaded from the barge onto the steamboat while both were moving! Other fuels were stocked; those that could make a roaring fire—turpentine, kerosene, pine pitch, even bacon fat—were highly prized.

Races such as the famous *Lee-Natchez* matchup were not uncommon along the river. And when boats raced, the danger of fire shot up. With overheated fireboxes down below, millions of fiery sparks would shoot up the smokestacks. Fire showers there could and sometimes did start boat fires.

One such fire broke out near Memphis during an 1832 race between the *Brandywine* and the *Hudson*. The *Brandywine* was behind in the race, so her crew poured resin into the firebox. Sparks landed on packing straw, causing an engine room fire. Soon the boat was completely engulfed. Before the fire was put out, more than 100 people, crew and passengers alike, died in the blaze.

During an 1837 race below Natchez, between the *Ben Sherrod* and the *Prairie*, a fire broke out in the engine

*Unfortunately, steamboat racing often resulted in disaster.*

room of the *Ben Sherrod*. Although the *Ben Sherrod's* pilot tried to get the boat to shore, which would allow passengers to escape, the fire burned through the ropes that connected the pilot's wheel to the ship's **rudder**. When the fire spread to several whiskey barrels, the liquor exploded into flames, sending the boat up with it. Finally the boat's boilers exploded. To top off the disaster, fire ignited 40 barrels of gunpowder. This explosion completely destroyed what was left of the *Ben Sherrod*.

But the tragedy was not yet over. Half an hour later a third boat, the *Columbus*, arrived. This boat slowed to help *Ben Sherrod* survivors out of the river. But another boat, the *Alton*, came around the bend, unaware of the tragedy, and plowed over many of the survivors. Others drowned in the boat's wake. One hundred fifty people died in this multiple accident.

And what about the *Prairie*, the other racing boat? Even after the fire had broken out aboard the *Ben Sherrod*, the captain of the *Prairie* kept going. However, he did manage to find the time to report the mishap when he arrived at his next docking.

Some steamboat tragedies involved boats that were racing to beat established speed records. One such case involved the *Moselle*. In 1838 this steamboat was one of the best and fastest along the Ohio River. On this particular voyage downriver to St. Louis, the boat's captain decided to attempt to beat the sailing record set by another boat. Speed was the order of the day, and even when Captain Perrin stopped in Cincinnati to take on passengers, he had the engineers keep the boilers roaring and the safety valves tied down.

As the *Moselle* left its **moorings** at Cincinnati, all four engine-room boilers exploded. The explosion was so severe that the boilers—and some human bodies as well—flew clear to the Kentucky side of the river, a distance of a quarter of a mile. Because of the thoughtless actions of Captain Perrin, 81 people died and another 55 were listed as missing.

Steamboats were destroyed in many other ways as well. Even when not racing, boilers blew up. This occurred especially in the early days of steamboating, before patented safety valves. There were the perils of the

★

water, including gravel bars and barrier reefs. And during the winter, ice floes threatened to smash the wooden hulls of the river steamers.

By 1856, near the end of the golden era of steamboating, an important insurance company listed the major and minor disasters that had happened on western rivers like the Mississippi, Ohio and others. The *Lloyd's Steamboat Directory* listed 87 major and 220 minor disasters involving steamboats. In each of the major mishaps, over 100 people had died. In the minor ones the death toll sometimes ran between 30 and 50. In less than 40 years of western steamboating—between 1811 and 1850—more than 4,000 people lost their lives in steamboat tragedies.

## The Famous *Robert E. Lee - Natchez* Race

Perhaps the most famous steamboat race was between the *Robert E. Lee* and the *Natchez*. For months these two steamboats had worked the Mississippi between New Orleans and St. Louis, but rarely on the same days. Finally the captain of the *Natchez* challenged the captain of the *Lee* to a race. The offer was accepted.

News about the planned race spread quickly. It even reached Europe along the Atlantic cable. During the weeks before the race, perhaps as much as $1 million was wagered on both sides concerning the race's outcome. Captain Leathers, perhaps overconfident, made no special changes to help his boat in the race. Rumor even had it that he had built this *Natchez*—the sixth boat to go by that name—just for this race with the *Lee*.

Captain Cannon of the *Lee* made many changes to his boat. He ordered all the glass removed from the boat's pilothouse, as well as all windows, shutters, doors and steam pipes that added weight and caused his boat to go slower. Other exterior weights, including booms, hoists, ropes and even the boat's anchor, were cast off to lighten the boat.

Finally the day of the big race arrived. It began at five o'clock in the afternoon. To help get a head start on the *Natchez*, the *Lee* was tied to the dock, its paddle wheel spinning. As the race began, with a pealing of the *Lee*'s big bell, a man on the dock swung an axe, cutting the straining *Lee* from its moorings. The boat quickly sped ahead of the *Natchez*, giving the *Lee* several minutes' head start. The *Natchez* never caught up.

When the *Lee* approached the city of Natchez, its citizens lined up along the docks. They were ready to cheer their **namesake**, but they watched in anger as another steamboat, the *Frank Pargoud*, came alongside the *Lee*. The two boats were tied together and wood was unloaded onto the *Lee* while both boats steamed along toward St. Louis.

But the *Natchez* would not be so easily outdone. The boat managed to give the *Lee* a run for its money. The outcome of the race was still in question as the boats approached the mouth of the Ohio, south of St. Louis. There the boats ran into a heavy fog. Despite the race, Captain Leathers tied up the *Natchez* and waited out the fog. Captain Cannon, along with his four handpicked pilots, kept going through the dangerous fog. Several times the *Lee* narrowly avoided crashing.

Finally on the Fourth of July, 1870, at 11:25 A.M., the *Robert E. Lee* sailed past the finish line along the St. Louis waterfront. Its official time: three days, 18 hours and 14 minutes. The *Natchez* finished the race on the same day, coming in six and a half hours later.

There were loud protests up and down the river regarding how the *Lee* had managed to win the race. Captain Cannon was accused of violating the rules of the race in using another steamboat to wood up. Some men

Many viewers lined up along the St. Louis waterfront on July 4, 1870, to watch the Robert E. Lee cross the finish line.

refused to pay off their lost bets because of the **shenanigans** of Captain Cannon. But the race had one other clear result: It marked the end of most of the steamboat racing along the Mississippi. Some said that Captain Cannon had taken the true spirit and fun out of the event.

And the handwriting was on the wall as well. Most of the steamboats along the Mississippi, the Ohio and even the Missouri were being replaced by the spread of the locomotive. Steam had moved from river to land, and the railroads could travel many places where steamboats could not. The Lee's race with the Natchez gave the winner its own set of gilded deer antlers. After that, however, few people seemed to care which boat boasted the once-important symbol.

★

Steamboats of today look very similar to those of the 1800s.
However, they are no longer relied upon as a major means
of transportation for Americans on the move.

# Steamboats
# of Today

Today steamboats can still be found on the western rivers. Some are used as museums that show the history of the important days of steamboating. Some carry river tourists up and down the Mississippi giving the people some idea of what steamboating was like long ago. In some western river cities steamboats now serve as floating gambling halls, with state-approved games of chance. Along the St. Louis waterfront fast-food chains operate restaurants on steamboats tied to the dock.

But the important period of western river steamboating, from 1811 to the beginning of the Civil War in 1861, is long past and nearly forgotten. Little is left of that exciting time of river travel in America except the rivers themselves—the Mississippi, Cumberland, Tennessee, Missouri, Arkansas and others—that continue to flow on as they always have.

# For Further Reading

Hartford, John. *Steamboat in a Cornfield*. New York: Crown Books, 1986.

Hult, Phil. *Whistles Around the Bend*. New York: Dodd Mead & Company, 1982.

McCall, Edith. *Mississippi Steamboatman: The Story of Henry Miller Shreve*. New York: Walker & Co., 1986.

Stein, Conrad R. *The Story of Mississippi Steamboats*. Chicago: Childrens Press, 1987.

Tunis, Edwin. *Oars, Sails and Steam: A Picture Book of Ships*. New York: HarperCollins, 1977.

# Glossary

**channel**—The deepest part of a river or strait.

**cord**—A unit of cut wood used for fuel, equal to a stack measuring 4-by-4-by-8-feet, or 128 cubic feet.

**crisscross**—To pass back and forth over something.

**fathom**—A unit of measure equal to six feet, often used in measuring the depth of water.

**forecastle**—The front part of the upper deck of a boat or ship.

**leadsman**—A roustabout who was responsible for using a knotted rope to determine the depth of water in which the steamboat was traveling.

**namesake**—One that has the same name as another.

**mooring**—A place where a boat has been tied up or secured.

**plantation**—A large farm that was often worked by black slaves.

**promenade**—A walkway running around the outside of a steamboat.

**roustabout**—A deckhand on a steamboat who would do manual labor such as loading and unloading cargo.

**rudder**—Piece of wood attached to the stern (back) of a boat which was used to guide or turn it.

**sawyer**—Logs or trees stuck in a river, so-called because the branches would saw back and forth with the current.

**shenanigan**—A trick used to fool someone.

**siege**—A military blockade of a city or fort designed to force a surrender.

**snag boat**—A specially-designed boat that cleared stumps and other obstacles from a river.

**spittoon**—A metal container for saliva. Also called a cuspidor.

**stateroom**—A private room or cabin on a boat or train.

**stoker**—Boiler room workers, often free blacks, who kept the boiler fire going by feeding it wood or coal.

# Index